For Emily, with love – KM
For Mum and Dad – KJ

STRIPES PUBLISHING
An imprint of Little Tiger Press
1 The Coda Centre, 189 Munster Road,
London SW6 6AW

A paperback original
First published in Great Britain in 2012

Text copyright © Kelly McKain, 2012
Illustrations copyright © Katy Jackson, 2012

ISBN: 978-1-84715-240-4

A CIP catalogue record for this book is available
from the British Library.

Printed and bound in the UK.

10 9 8 7 6 5 4 3 2 1

ANIMAL S.O.S.

THE MYSTERY OF THE CLIFF-TOP DOG

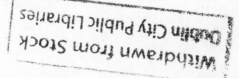

ANIMAL S.O.S.

THE MYSTERY OF THE CLIFF-TOP DOG

KELLY McKAIN

Illustrated by Katy Jackson

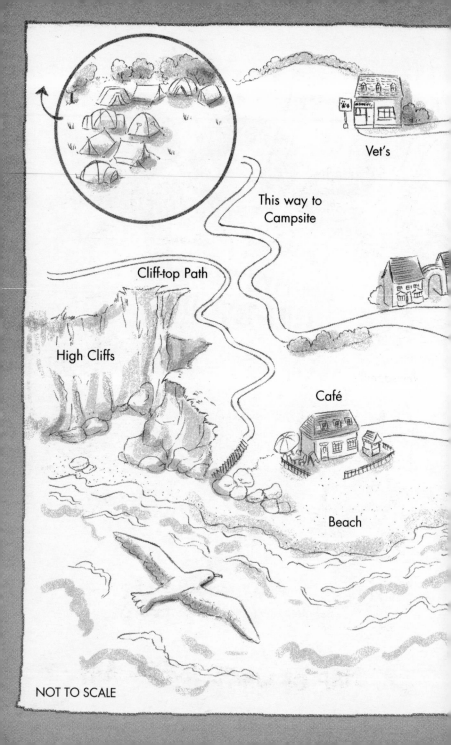

Vet's

This way to
Campsite

Cliff-top Path

High Cliffs

Café

Beach

NOT TO SCALE

CHAPTER ONE

The beach was beautiful, with pristine sand, and the sun glimmered on the water. There was a fresh breeze and Amy was glad she'd worn her padded jacket. She pulled her long blonde hair back into a ponytail, and found herself a good spot to sit down and do some sketching while she waited for Mum to join her.

She'd been coming to the beach every day since they had arrived at White Horse Bay, a week ago. She was getting to like the small Cornish fishing village. She loved exploring

its narrow, winding streets or sitting with
Mum on the harbour wall, eating ice creams
and watching the little boats come and go.

It still felt like they were on holiday,
though – she couldn't imagine the B&B
Mum had bought actually being her home.
Especially not once the builders had
finished, and there were guests coming and
going all the time. To Amy, home was
London. Home was traffic and bustle and
museums and shops. And Dino's Italian
restaurant, of course.

She and Dad would often head over
there when he got in from work. Even
though her parents had split up years
before, Dad had always lived round the
corner. Amy had her own room in his flat
and she used to spend almost half her time
there. Now she'd only be staying with him
one weekend a month. He'd promised to
visit her whenever he could, but still, they'd

have far less time together. That would take some getting used to.

"I live in White Horse Bay," Amy said aloud to herself. But it still didn't seem real. She couldn't stop thinking about Lucy and Aisha, her best friends from school – well, her old school. She'd still be able to meet up with them when she visited Dad, but it wouldn't be the same. She wasn't starting at her new school, where she'd be a weekly boarder, until after the Easter holidays. And she hadn't seen anyone her own age around the village yet, either.

But Amy didn't mind – not that much, anyway. She was having her first riding lesson that afternoon. Just thinking about it made her stomach flip with excitement. Amy loved animals and she'd been into ponies for as long as she could remember. She had loads of books about them and read *Pony* magazine, but she'd never actually got the chance to ride. She was always so busy in London, with after-school clubs, sleepovers and cinema trips with her friends. Then there were visits to art galleries with Dad, and shopping with Mum, of course.

When her mum announced the big move, it had come as a complete shock to Amy, and she hadn't wanted to leave. The riding lessons were the only good thing she could see about leaving behind everyone and everything she knew. Mum had suggested them – it was her way of trying to cheer Amy up. Amy wondered what the instructor would be like (not too strict, she hoped!) and what kind of pony she'd get to ride. She couldn't help smiling to herself as she checked her watch. Today, in precisely two hours and forty-two minutes, she was going to be riding for the very first time.

Amy found a clean page in her sketchbook and took a pencil from her pencil box. It had been a gift from Dad just before she'd left London. They'd had the longest hug, and she knew he'd miss her just as much as she'd miss him.

There weren't too many tourists around, not this early in the season, so the beach was the perfect place for sketching dogs. She began to draw one of the Labs that was bouncing around in the sea, when…

DOOOOOOF!

Suddenly, there was a big wet nose in her face and huge paws on her jeans, and she was knocked backwards into the sand.

Her pencils scattered in all directions and
her sketchbook went flying.

"Oh, hello, boy!" she cried, pulling
herself up. "Where did you come from?"
The big shaggy brown dog looked like a
cross between a retriever and something
scruffier. She ruffled his fur, and he panted
happily and tried to lick her face.

"Rufus! Come here!" A girl came hurrying
over, wearing denim cut-offs and a checked
shirt despite the cold wind. Her brown wavy
hair was blowing all over the place.

The girl grinned at Amy. "Sorry! He *has* been to training, but none of it sank in!"

"I don't mind," Amy insisted, rubbing the dog's ears. She was happy to be talking to someone her own age at last. "He's gorgeous! I'd love a dog."

"You should get one, then," said the girl, as if it was that simple.

Amy frowned. "I'm working on my mum. But it's not going to be easy! She's not exactly an animal person. I'm Amy, by the way."

The girl grinned at her again. "I'm Leah. And this dufus ... is Rufus!"

Amy gave Rufus another big pat, and he lay down on the sand and rolled on to his back so she could stroke his tummy.

"What kind of dog would you like?" Leah asked.

Amy didn't hesitate. "Well, it would have to be energetic enough to take for long walks, but small enough to curl up with on the sofa," she said. "Maybe a Jack Russell, or a clever mongrel with bags of personality – a rescued one so I could give it a lovely new home…"

"Rufus is a rescue dog," said Leah proudly. "I haven't seen you before. Are you on holiday?"

"We've just moved down from London," Amy explained. "My mum's opening a B&B."

"Oh, right," said Leah. "It must seem a bit boring round here, then!"

Amy smiled. "Not really, just different."

She leaned over to pick up her scattered pencils. Leah knelt down to help, and peered at her sketchbook. "Wow! These are really good!"

Amy blushed and mumbled, "Thanks."

Then Rufus leaped up, and began barking and bouncing about. "Gotta go," said Leah. "I promised Ru we'd go right round the bay to climb on the rocks!"

"Oh, OK. Bye," said Amy. "Hey, I wonder—" she began, but Leah and Rufus were already bounding off towards the cliffs. She'd wanted to ask whether Leah fancied meeting up some time, and now she'd missed her chance. Still, maybe she'd see her around.

She picked up her sketchbook again. The Labs were far away down the beach now. There was an old St Bernard loping along next to his owner, but she'd drawn him before, so instead she started on a plucky little terrier chasing a ball.

"Amy! Amy!"

Amy turned to see Mum stumbling across the sand in her high heels, carrying a picnic basket. She smiled and waved.

It looked like Mum still needed to adjust to life by the sea, too – starting with buying some sensible shoes!

After their picnic, Mum drove Amy to her riding lesson. Amy's stomach flipped again when she saw the sign for White Horse Stables. By the time they pulled into the ramshackle farmyard, she was so excited she couldn't stop grinning. There were a few ponies grazing in the field beside the car park, and she wondered whether one of them would be hers. As they made their way over to the yard, a tall, tousle-haired man strode up to greet them.

"Hi, you must be Amy!" he said cheerily.

"Yes, and this is my mum," she said.

The man gave them a warm smile. "I'm Dan. My wife, Rosie, and I run this place. I mainly manage the yard, but I do a bit of instructing and take visitors out on hacks, too. So, feeling excited, Amy?"

Amy nodded. "Yes, very! I've never ridden before, though, so I haven't got a hat or the right boots or anything…"

Dan grinned at her and gestured to a low building in the corner of the yard. "Not to worry, we've got plenty of spares in the yard office. You head on in there and get yourself kitted out. Rosie is expecting you. She'll be teaching you today on Nutmeg. Have a great time." He turned to Mum. "Feel free to stay and watch."

"Thanks," they both said. Then he smiled and strolled away.

Mum gave Amy a hug. "Good luck. I know you'll be brilliant. I'll go and stand by the fence. Unless me watching is going to make you too nervous, of course."

"No, it would be nice to have you there," Amy insisted. She suddenly felt a pang of nerves. "You can come and pick me up when I get thrown off," she added.

"You'll be fine, sweetheart," Mum reassured her.

"I hope so!" said Amy. "Right, let's go for it." She headed over to the yard office, but as she reached the doorway she stopped still. There was some kind of argument going on. Then, with a start, she realized that the row was about her.

"But, Mum, why does she have to ride Nutmeg?" a girl moaned. "I was planning to take him out for a hack this afternoon!"

18

"You know why," said a woman. Amy thought that it must be Rosie. "He's nice and steady—"

"So's Gracie," the girl protested.

Rosie sighed. "Gracie's had two lessons already today, and with the group hack later on, it'll be too much for her."

She looked up sharply, catching sight of Amy. "Oh, hello! It's Amy, isn't it?" she asked, smiling. "Welcome to White Horse Stables."

The girl with her turned round, and Amy gasped. It was Leah! So Rosie and Dan were her parents. This was her home.

"Hi!" Amy said brightly. But to her surprise, Leah just muttered something about finishing the mucking out, then marched past her and stormed off across the yard.

"Don't worry about her," said Rosie. "She just got out of the wrong side of bed this morning. Let's find you some gear."

Amy felt excited and nervous all at once when Rosie's teenage son, George, led Nutmeg out for her. He was a gorgeous chestnut pony with a thick, unruly mane and clumpy feet. He hadn't seemed that big, but once Amy was in the saddle she felt very high up. Rosie showed her how to hold the reins and helped her to adjust her stirrups, and then they were off.

"Oh!" she gasped, as Nutmeg started walking towards the manège, with George keeping hold of the lead rein. It was a really strange feeling and with every step she felt like she was going to slide off.

"Keep looking forward, and concentrate on sitting up tall and keeping your heels down," said Rosie. "That will help you to balance. And you can hold on to the front of the saddle, too, if you feel really unsteady."

Amy nodded and tried hard to remember everything. After a few minutes in the saddle, she was getting used to the way Nutmeg moved. She'd even stopped glancing down at the ground all the time.

"Now, let's think about going forward to halt," Rosie called. "Shorten your reins a fraction, and then sit up tall and give a gentle pull." As Nutmeg came to a stop she said, "That's it. Well done."

"I can't believe I made him halt!" cried Amy in delight.

After a few more tries at going from walk

to halt and back to walk, Rosie called,
"I think you could have a go at trot, if
you'd like to."

"Yes, please!" said Amy.

When Nutmeg started trotting, Amy
really did think she was going to fall off!
But then Rosie showed her how to sit
deeply into the saddle so that she didn't
bounce around so much, and soon she got
into a rhythm and felt much more stable.

"Right, time to come off the lead rein,
I think," Rosie said then, and Amy beamed.

"Well done, darling!" Mum called out.

"Thanks! That was amazing!" Amy cried, as Rosie showed her how to dismount at the end of the lesson. After taking Nutmeg round the manège all by herself several times, she felt like a real rider! She made a big fuss of him, ruffling his mane and stroking his nose.

Rosie grinned. "You're a natural – your balance is excellent," she told her.

Amy couldn't help smiling. "Maybe it's because I used to do gymnastics at my old school," she said.

"Yes, that would definitely help," said Rosie, "but you've got a lovely way with ponies, too. Nutmeg felt as easy with you as you did with him."

Amy gave the gorgeous pony a final pat and stroke, and as Rosie led him away to the stables, Mum rushed over and hugged her.

"Did you enjoy yourself?" she asked.

Amy grinned. "It was great," she said.
"I definitely want to come back again.
How about tomorrow?"

"I'll see if they've got a space free next
week," Mum told her. "Until the B&B is
up and running we're on a bit of a tight
budget, I'm afraid. It's brilliant that you
liked it, though. Oh, and I noticed a girl
walking across the yard earlier. She looked
about your age. Did you see her?"

Amy frowned, thinking of Leah. "Yes,
she's Rosie and Dan's daughter," she
muttered.

Mum smiled. "So she lives here. Even
better, then! Maybe you could invite her
over? I know you'll make new friends when
school starts, but it would be nice to know
someone locally, wouldn't it?"

"Hmm." Amy pretended to be very
interested in undoing her riding hat. She

had hoped to get to know Leah after they'd met on the beach. But now, having seen how moody she'd been over Nutmeg, she wasn't so keen to make friends.

"Leah, you know it wasn't Amy's fault she had to ride Nutmeg," said Rosie. Amy and her mum had just left, and Rosie was leaning on Nutmeg's stable door as Leah untacked him.

"I know," Leah said. "I just really wanted to take him on a long ride this afternoon. I hardly ever get the chance—"

"We have to put the clients first, you know that," Rosie cut in. "You can't just pick and choose when you ride."

Leah undid Nutmeg's girth and put it carefully up on top of the saddle. "It wasn't anything against her," she mumbled.

"Well, when she comes next time I'd like

you to apologize," Rosie said sternly. "Amy loved her lesson, she was great with Nutmeg and she tried really hard, too. I don't want her to feel she isn't welcome here. OK?"

"OK," Leah muttered. "Sorry, Mum."

"Good," said Rosie. "There's some chocolate cake in the kitchen," she added, softening. "You might want to get in and have some before your brothers spot it."

"Thanks, Mum," Leah called, as Rosie strode away.

Leah pulled off Nutmeg's saddle and hung it over the stable door. Nutmeg whinnied and gave her a stern look, almost as stern as Rosie's.

"I know," she told him, wincing. "I shouldn't have taken it out on Amy. She seems really nice and, oh…" She sighed deeply, thinking of what a rotten welcome to White Horse Stables she'd given her. "I've been awful, haven't I?"

Nutmeg nudged her sleeve softly. That meant yes, Leah decided.

"I'll make sure I'm extra friendly to Amy at her next lesson," she resolved. "Come on, I'll get you turned out and then grab some of that cake before making up the teatime feeds."

CHAPTER TWO

"Yum!" Amy declared, as she finished her huge jacket potato with cheese. "Now, how about dessert?"

"I don't know where you put it all!" said Mum, laughing.

They were having lunch at the Beach Café. It was Mum's treat, to make up for dragging Amy round the bathroom store in Castlereach, the nearest town, all morning.

The café was buzzing with a mix of visitors and mums with pushchairs. Mrs Penhale, the owner, was behind the counter, arranging some freshly-baked chocolate muffins. Her husband was bringing in the tables from the patio.

Amy looked up at the darkening sky. "Is there a storm coming?" she asked, as Mr Penhale came back inside.

He nodded. "A big one, according to the weather report."

Mum shuddered and finished up her coffee. "Let's get back to the B&B before it starts raining."

"Mr Penhale, according to the weather report, have I got time for a chocolate muffin?" Amy asked with a grin.

"Oh, yes, I think so," he told her, smiling back.

"Go on, then," said Mum. "But if this suede jacket gets ruined in the rain, I'm holding you responsible!"

After Amy had polished off one of the giant chocolate muffins, she and Mum made their way along the beach to the B&B. They were nearly at the steps up to the harbour when Amy realized that she'd left her jacket on the back of her chair. "I'll just run and get it," she told Mum. "You carry on, I won't be a minute."

She hurried back to the café and found that Mrs Penhale had put it safely on a peg in the stockroom for her. And it was on her way back along the beach that she heard it.

The strange noise.

Amy froze, listening carefully. There it was again – a faint cry, like a whimper, on the wind. It seemed to be coming from over by the cliffs. She peered up at them and – oh! She'd spotted something, she was sure of it – a flash of golden-brown part way up, on a jagged ledge. It could have been an old T-shirt or a plastic bag, of course. But with that noise as well… What if it was an animal? And what if it was trapped?

She stared hard at the ledge, but she couldn't see anything now. And the noise had stopped, too. Still, she ought to try and get a better look. She'd just have to tell Mum where she was going first.

Amy was surprised to find Mum exactly where she'd left her, and now she was talking to a girl on a pony. As she neared them, she could see it was Leah and Nutmeg.

Mum beamed at her as she approached. "Amy, there you are. I was just telling … Leah, isn't it?" Leah nodded, then gave Amy an uncomfortable glance. "Leah, that she should come round to play—"

"Mum!" Amy protested.

"Oh, sorry," Mum giggled. "Not *play*, you're far too old for that. *Hang out* with you sometime. I could take you into Castlereach for pizza, or you could watch a DVD. That would be fun, wouldn't it?"

When neither of the girls said anything to that, she added, "Even better, why don't you two do something now?"

"Fine with me," said Leah.

"But I—" Amy began.

"Only keep away from the cliffs, won't you, sweetheart?" Mum added. She frowned at the darkening sky. "It looks like the storm Mr Penhale mentioned is on its way. If you get caught out, you can always both come back to the B&B." She flashed a smile at Leah. "Though I'm not sure what we'd do with the pony!" Then she turned to Amy again. "You've got your phone, haven't you?"

Amy nodded and patted her jacket pocket.

"Charged up?"

She nodded again.

"Good. Well, I'll see you later, then."

"Erm, hang on—" Amy said, as Mum strode off. She'd wanted to tell her about the strange noise, and get her to come back along the beach and listen out for it, too, but Mum was already hurrying away.

"Sorry about her. I've got to go," Amy said shortly, and set off after Mum.

"Wait, please," Leah called.

Amy sighed and crossed her arms. She didn't really want to talk to Leah, not after what had happened at the stables. "What is it?" she muttered.

Leah dismounted and followed after Amy, leading Nutmeg. "Amy, I'm sorry about yesterday," she said. "I shouldn't have been so mean."

Amy couldn't help smiling. Leah sounded like she meant it, and there was no point holding silly grudges. "That's OK," she said.

Just then, she heard the noise again. It was much fainter from here, but now it really did sound like the desperate whine of an animal in distress. She gripped Leah's arm. "Listen. Can you hear it?"

Leah frowned and craned her neck towards the cliffs. "You mean that sort-of whimpering?" she asked.

"Yes. It's an animal, I'm sure of it now. When I was walking back from the café I heard something up on the cliffs, and—"

She didn't have to say any more. Leah was back on Nutmeg in a flash. "Come on, let's go and investigate!" she said, and with

that she and Nutmeg set off across the
sand at a brisk trot.

As Amy dashed after them, a huge knot
formed in her stomach. Would they even be
able to reach the animal? And what if they
did? Would they be able to help?

The girls made their way along the beach,
looking up at the cliffs as they went.
But they couldn't see anything and
the whimpering sound seemed to have
stopped.

"We'll have a much better view from the cliff top," Leah reasoned.

Amy hesitated. The sky had darkened even more and black clouds were gathering menacingly above them. "I don't know," she said. "My mum—"

"We're only going along the top path to have a quick look," Leah put in. "We'll be long gone by the time the storm breaks."

Amy still wasn't sure – to her it looked like the clouds were about to burst at any moment. But there was an animal up there, she was sure of it. Something frightened and maybe injured… They couldn't just leave it, could they? "OK, let's go for it," she said.

Leah dismounted and they made their way up the steep path that ran from the beach to the cliffs. The only people they passed were heading back down. About halfway up, a portly man in a wax jacket and a battered old hat stopped to give Nutmeg a pat.

"Hi, Bernard," said Leah. "This is Amy. She's new to White Horse Bay."

"Hello, and welcome," said Bernard gruffly, tipping his hat.

Amy smiled. "Thanks."

"If there's anything you want to know about the village, Bernard's a good person to ask," Leah told her. "He knows everything about everything."

"I wouldn't say that!" said Bernard, smiling slightly, "but I do have an interest in local history." Then he waved up at the cliffs. "Don't be long up there, will you, girls," he warned.

Leah smiled. "Of course not," she said. "I'm quickly showing Amy the view."

"Well, stay away from the top path. It gets so slippery in heavy rain."

Leah just nodded.

As they said goodbye and continued up
the cliff path, Amy's mind was whirring.
If a local had warned them not to go along
the cliff top with the storm coming, then
clearly it really was dangerous. "Are you
sure we should be doing this?" she asked
Leah nervously.

"No," Leah admitted. "But what choice
do we have?"

Amy sighed. "You're right. We can't leave
an animal in danger. Let's be as quick as

we can, though. Mum would go mad if she knew I was up here."

They picked their way along the narrow path, right by the crumbling, craggy cliff edge. Every few paces they stopped, and Amy peered over. But there was nothing, only jagged rocks and craggy ledges and scrubby bushes.

Leah was still leading Nutmeg, and as the path petered to a tiny trail, the brave little pony scrambled over the rocky parts, stumbling in places and sending small rocks bouncing down behind him. Just then, there was a loud rumble of thunder, which made him leap backwards and whinny. "Hush, boy, it's all right," Leah said soothingly.

"We haven't heard the noise for ages," said Amy. "Maybe we've come too far. I think we should head back."

Leah frowned. "Let's go a little further, just in case."

"OK," said Amy, feeling more worried with every second that passed.

Rain began to spatter the path, speckling the yellow dirt on the narrow trail as they edged along it in single file. Suddenly, Amy grabbed Leah's arm. "Wait! There! I think I heard it."

Both girls stood completely still, listening.

There was the forlorn whining sound again. And it seemed to be coming from the cliff face directly below them.

Amy knelt down and leaned over the edge as far as she could. She scanned the crags and crevices, desperately searching for the source of the noise.

Then she saw it – huddled into the scrub on a jagged ledge about halfway down. "Oh no, Leah, it's a dog!" she cried.

Leah gasped. "The poor thing! Does it look OK?"

Amy lay down on her tummy and leaned over. "He's a cocker spaniel," she said. "A young one. He's obviously frightened. And from the way he's holding his paw, he could be injured, too. I'm going down."

"Be careful," Leah said, clutching Nutmeg's lead rope tight.

Amy's heart was pounding as she wiped the splashes of rain from her face and did up her jacket. She swung her legs carefully over the cliff edge and hung by her fingers for a moment, then dropped on to the closest ledge. She crawled along through the gorse and over the crumbled rock. Then there was another drop. She swung down again and scrabbled for her next foothold, but it was out of reach. She couldn't risk

letting herself drop too far, in case she lost
her footing when she landed. The cliff was
at least as high as a house, and so steep she
knew she could easily end up tumbling all
the way to the bottom. The spaniel was
watching her and whimpered again. Amy
felt awful letting the dog down, but it was
just impossible.

"Amy, what's happening?" Leah said
anxiously.

"It's too difficult. I'll have to come back
up!" Amy called. She scrambled for a
foothold to haul herself on to the nearest
ledge, but the rock just crumbled away
under her feet. Her heart pounding, she
finally got a tiny toehold and managed to
heave herself up. She clambered back up
the cliff and pulled herself on to the path,
panting for breath.

"Can I use your phone to call home?"
asked Leah. "We can't do this on our own."

Amy fumbled for her mobile, and Leah tried both her house and the yard office, but there was no answer at either.

Amy frowned. "I don't think I can call *my* mum," she said. "She'll go mad if she finds out we've been up on the cliffs... And besides, I can't see *her* scrambling down there. She'll just insist on calling the coastguard or something."

"Oh, that's a point. We can call the coastguard ourselves," said Leah. "My mum made us all learn the number off by heart," she added, as she dialled. She got an answer immediately and explained in a breathless voice about the injured dog and the cliff. Then she said, "Yes, but..." a lot and hung up.

She sighed and handed back the phone.

"Well?" said Amy eagerly.

"It was Tom Trescothick – he's a friend of Dad's. He's been part of the team for years,"

Leah told her. "He wanted to help, but there's a tourist boat in trouble in Sandy Cove, round the rocks, and they won't have a team free for hours yet."

Amy's heart sank. "But you told them the dog was injured, I heard you!" she cried. "It's like they don't care!"

"They do," Leah insisted. "But Tom was far more worried about *us* getting down from here before the storm breaks. Hey, that's given me an idea. Maybe I can get up from the base of the cliff and reach the dog that way. I've done quite a bit of climbing. Not up to that height, but…"

Amy frowned. The rain was getting harder, and the thunder was rumbling above them again. Trying to climb up the cliff sounded just as crazy as trying to climb down it. She leaned over the edge again and searched for the dog. There he was, licking his paw and shivering in the rain. He was weak, cold, and in need of food and water.

"Oh!" she gasped, as he laid down his head and closed his eyes. He seemed to be giving up. She wondered who he belonged to, and where his owner was now. There was certainly no one else around. They really were his only hope. And if Leah thought she could climb up and reach him, well, they had to try, didn't they?

"Amy?" Leah prompted. "What do you reckon?"

"It's dangerous, but time's running out," Amy told her. "We have to rescue that dog, and fast!"

CHAPTER THREE

"The storm's coming, we have to hurry!" yelled Leah, as she and Amy stumbled down the main cliff path, which was now slick with rain. Nutmeg whinnied anxiously as his hooves slipped and skidded. And when the lightning crackled above them, the poor pony went skittering backwards, jerking on his lead rope and pulling Leah with him.

Amy shuddered as thunder rolled around the sky. She was cold and wet, and every bone in her body was telling her that they should just get home as quickly as possible. But she knew they couldn't do that. As they finally reached the bottom of the path, she lurched across the sand after Leah.

Heads down against the pelting rain and fierce wind, they trekked to the spot where they'd seen the dog.

"This is the place," Amy cried. "Look, there's that big scrubby bush."

Leah scanned the cliff face directly below the bush, shielding her eyes from the rain. "Yes, and there's the ledge," she said. "It's higher than it looked when we were at the top."

Amy frowned. It did look very high. It was a steep climb, too. "Are you sure about this?" she asked.

Leah just handed her Nutmeg's lead rope and grimaced. "Not really, but what choice do we have? Wish me luck."

"Good luck," whispered Amy.

She got as close to the base of the cliff as she could, and watched anxiously. Leah had scrambled over the rocks at the bottom quite easily, but now she needed to make the steep ascent.

Amy held her breath as Leah threw herself forward and grabbed for a tiny bit of scrub. She couldn't believe it would hold Leah's weight. But although it bent right over, it didn't break – phew! She felt sick. She knew they were in the right place, but the dog wasn't whining any more. Leah was doing her best, clinging to whatever bit of rock or scrub she could and scrabbling up, higher and higher. She was nearly halfway now. But maybe it was already too late…

With another huge flash of lightning, the rain started to lash down even harder. Nutmeg pranced around and whinnied.

Amy's soaking fingers slipped on the wet lead rope and she nearly lost her grip. She stroked his neck gently and whispered, "It's all right, Nutmeg. Nothing's going to hurt you."

She stared anxiously at the figure of her new friend, clinging on to the cliff face. She realized now that they were way out of their depth. What if Leah slipped? She was about as high as the roof of a house. If she fell from there ... well, Amy couldn't bring herself to think about it. Nutmeg nudged her sleeve. He looked as scared as she did. "Don't worry, Leah will be OK," she told him, even though she wasn't sure she believed it herself.

Leah had her fingers on the ledge where the dog was now, but...

"AAAAHHHHH!" she cried, as she lost her foothold. She hung in the air, her eyes filled with terror.

Amy's heart was pounding so hard she felt like it was going to burst. But she had to keep her head for her friend's sake, and the dog's.

"There's a rock not too far away from your left foot. If you stretch you could reach it," Amy shouted. "Go on, Leah. You can make it!"

Amy watched as Leah swung her body backwards and lifted her legs, but she missed the outcrop and smashed against the cliff. "Come on, try again!" Amy called, doing her best to sound confident. "Swing out a little more this time!"

"I can't!" Leah screamed. "My fingers are slipping. I'm going to fall!"

"You can do it, I know you can!" Amy shouted.

Just then, a streak of lightning and boom of thunder sent Nutmeg springing backwards, nearly pulling Amy over.

The lead rope slipped from her fingers, but she managed to grab his bridle.

Leah let out a loud cry as she swung backwards, then stretched out her legs for the outcrop. Her toes just brushed it and she fought for a foothold.

"Yes, you've got it!" Amy called. "Now, pull! Pull yourself up!"

With another huge cry, Leah dragged herself on to the ledge and collapsed in a heap. She rolled round to look down at Amy. "He's here!" she shouted, then vanished from view again.

Amy threw her arms round Nutmeg's neck, feeling sick with relief.

"Come here, boy, it's OK," said Leah softly, still panting for breath. "I've come to rescue you – you can trust me."

With his last ounce of strength, the little

dog gave a yelp and fell into her trembling arms. "Right, let's get you down," she whispered. She shuffled towards the edge of the ledge.

It was then that she realized she had a big problem. She needed both hands to get back down the cliff.

"Amy, I can't climb with the dog in my arms!" she shouted, feeling panic rise in her chest. "What am I going to do?"

"I don't know!" Amy cried, her mind racing. "How about … can you tuck the dog inside your jumper?"

Leah shook her head. "He's too big." Why hadn't she thought of this? "Now we're both stuck!" she shouted. "I'm not coming down without him!"

Suddenly, an idea popped into Amy's head. "We could use Nutmeg's bridle as a harness and lower him down," she called, pushing her dripping hair from her eyes. "If you can get him to the bottom of the cliff, you can climb down and then carry him over the lower rocks."

Leah thought for a moment. "It's a long shot, but it might just work," she shouted. "Let's give it a go. You'll need to put the lead rope loosely round his neck to hold him once you've taken the bridle off. Can you do that?"

"I think so," said Amy. She unclipped the lead rope and put it round Nutmeg's neck, but then, when she went to take off the bridle, it suddenly looked really complicated, with loads of buckles and straps. "I don't know how to get it off!" she cried.

Leah called out step-by-step instructions, telling Amy which buckles to undo and how to draw it over Nutmeg's head. That left her holding him only by the lead rope. Amy was more worried than ever that he'd bolt off and hurt himself, but she tried to stay calm. She led Nutmeg over as many of the low rocks as she was able to, to get as close to the cliff as possible. "Ready?" she shouted.

Leah carefully placed the dog on the ledge. Then she lay flat out, with her arms outstretched. "Ready!" she called.

Amy took a deep breath. She'd wrapped the reins round the bridle to make it as much of a ball shape as possible, so it would be easier to throw, but still it seemed a very long way up. "One, two, three, catch!" she yelled, and hurled the bridle as hard as she could up to Leah.

The bridle hit the ledge and then seemed to bounce away, jangling. Leah lunged for it, and nearly went tumbling down the cliff. In a split second, she grabbed for a patch of scrub with one hand and reached out for the bridle with the other. Her fingers brushed the edge of one of the reins and she just managed to grab hold.

"Yes! Good catch!" Amy shouted.

Leah grinned. "Good throw!" She gently strapped the bridle round the dog, putting the noseband over his neck and the brow band round his middle, talking to him gently the whole time. She expected him to wriggle or whine, but he was worryingly still and quiet. Then she undid one end of the reins from the bit, to make it as long as possible.

"Right, going down!" she said, leaning as far over as she could. Slowly and carefully, she began to lower the dog towards the ground. The reins were long enough … just. The dog landed gently on the low rocks and she let go.

The little dog lay still as Leah scrambled down. Amy was desperate to go over and pick him up, but she couldn't risk leaving Nutmeg. "Hurry up, Leah," she whispered to herself. "Every second counts!"

Leah scrambled back down the cliff face. Once she reached the low rocks she scooped the dog up, threw the long rein over her arm, and stumbled back to Amy.

"Well done, that was amazing," Amy gasped, as she carefully took the dog from her friend.

Leah grinned as she unbuckled the bridle and lifted the dog out of it. "I didn't think we'd get down from there – good thinking about the bridle!" she told Amy.

Leah took Nutmeg's lead rope from her and quickly put his bridle back on, then she put on her riding hat and mounted up. Meanwhile, Amy pulled off her jacket, wrapped the dog up in it and cuddled him close.

"Let's go and take shelter in the café!"
Leah cried, as another round of thunder
and lightning shattered the sky.

Then she and Nutmeg set off at a canter,
with Amy running behind them, the
shivering dog safe inside her jacket.

CHAPTER FOUR

Leah tied Nutmeg up outside the Beach Café. When the girls trooped inside, soaking wet and covered in mud, Mrs Penhale looked up and stared.

"My goodness, what on earth happened to you two?" she gasped, rushing over. Then she caught sight of the bedraggled dog swaddled in Amy's jacket. "And who's this little fellow?" she cried, stroking his soggy ears.

"We don't know," said Leah. "We rescued him from the cliffs."

"We know he could do with some food, though," added Amy. She rummaged in her skirt pocket for some change. "Can I buy a chicken sandwich?"

But Mrs Penhale wouldn't take a penny. She rushed to get the dog a bowl of water, and a big helping of chicken from the fridge. Then Mr Penhale steered the girls to a table and insisted on making them both big mugs of hot chocolate.

"Thanks so much, this is delicious," Amy told him, as she sipped her drink. She was soaked through and the steaming, velvety hot chocolate was just what she needed. She knew Leah was feeling the same, because she was cupping the mug in her scratched, muddy hands and sipping happily.

Meanwhile, the dog had eaten all his food and was beginning to look more alert. Amy gave him a stroke and he jumped up and tried to lick her face, but his sore leg made him yelp with pain.

"Ouch, nasty paw you've got there, little one," said Mrs Penhale, who'd come over with second helpings for him.

"It does look bad, doesn't it?" said Leah. "It's really swollen." She turned to Amy. "I think we should take him to the vet's to get him checked over as soon as the rain's eased off. My cousin Kate works there on reception and Mr Ellis, the vet, is really nice. He was brilliant with our cat, Tiger, when he was ill last year."

Amy stroked the dog as Leah gently rubbed him dry with the hand towel Mr Penhale had given her.

"It feels funny, just calling him 'the dog'," Leah said. "There's no tag on his collar. Shall we make up a name for him? Only until we find his owners, of course."

Amy tickled the dog under the chin and he licked her hand. "How about calling him Scamp, for now?" she suggested. "He must have scampered down the cliff before he fell. And when that paw gets better he'll be scampering round again, won't you, boy?"

The dog nuzzled into her T-shirt and she ruffled his fur.

Leah grinned. "Scamp. It suits him!"

Mr Penhale wandered back over. "Did you say he was lost?" he asked.

The girls nodded.

"You know, a teenage boy came in early this morning," he said. "He asked if we'd heard anything about a dog being found. I said we hadn't, and offered to take his details and call him if I did. But the funny thing was, I went to get a pad and pen, and when I came back he'd gone."

"That *is* strange," said Leah. "Can you remember anything about him?"

Mr Penhale thought for a moment. "He was wearing a red jacket. And there was another lad in glasses and a girl waiting round the side of the café for him. They would have been about fifteen or sixteen."

"Why would he leave before you could take his number?" Amy wondered.

"People don't always think straight when they're upset," said Mrs Penhale, stroking the dog's head. "He was probably just anxious to get on to the next place."

"Probably," said Amy. "And you never know, maybe he stopped in at the vet's as well, and *did* remember to leave his number that time." She gasped. "Oh, I'd better call Mum. She might be wondering where I've got to."

She pulled her phone from her jacket and blinked at it. "Oh no! I've got five missed calls from her," she said, frowning. "I didn't even hear my phone ring."

Amy called Mum back straight away and explained what had happened. She missed out the bit about them going up on the cliffs because she thought it would be better to confess that later, when they were face to face. "We're going to take him to get checked over now," she finished. "Leah knows the vet."

Mum tried to make Amy come back to the B&B first to get changed into something warm and dry, but Amy insisted that she

was OK, and that getting Scamp looked
at was much more important. So eventually
Mum agreed. When Mr Penhale heard
that the girls were planning to head
straight for the vet's, he went and got
towels for them, too, so they could dry their
hair off at least.

Once the rain slowed, Amy and Leah
headed up through the main village
and climbed the steep, narrow street to
the vet's surgery. Leah led Nutmeg and
Amy carried Scamp, still wrapped up
in her jacket.

Soon they were in the cosy reception,
with Nutmeg tied up out the back,
munching the grass. As Kate listened to
their story, she made a big fuss of Scamp
and fed him dog treats from a jar on the
counter. "You're in luck," she told the girls.

"Mr Ellis is with his last patient of the clinic, and this cute little face should persuade him to take just one more."

"Has anyone been in about a missing dog?" Amy asked.

"No, no one," Kate said, but then she thought for a moment. "Actually, there was a phone call around lunchtime. A girl wanted to know if a dog had been brought in, but when I asked for a detailed description of it, and her name and phone number, she hung up."

ANIMAL S.O.S.

Amy and Leah looked at each other. Something was definitely odd about that.

"If I were looking for a dog, I'd do everything I could and give as much information as possible," said Amy.

"Yeah, if it was Rufus, I'd go to the ends of the earth," Leah insisted.

"Kate, do you think it's strange that no one was on the cliff top looking for Scamp?" Amy asked.

"Perhaps that isn't where he got lost," Kate reasoned. "He could have gone off after a scent and not been able to find his way back."

"True," said Leah. "I still think it's a bit weird, though. There seem to be three teenagers looking for him, but not wanting anyone to know who they are. I can understand being too upset to remember to leave your details once, but to do it twice looks deliberate."

"I agree," said Amy. "I wonder why, though?"

Just then, Mr Ellis came into reception. He strode over to the girls and said hello, then stroked Scamp's ears. "Who's this lovely little chap?" he asked, tickling him under the chin. "You look like you've been in the wars – all three of you!"

Kate explained about Scamp being stuck on the cliff. "Sounds like you had a narrow escape!" Mr Ellis told the little dog. "Come on, then, let's have a look at you."

They went through to his consulting room and he gave Scamp a good check over, while the girls waited anxiously.

"Well, I'm pleased to say there are no internal injuries," he told them.

"Oh, thank goodness!" Amy gasped.

"And no broken bones, either," the vet continued. "He's got off lightly, considering how far he must have fallen. His paw is very bruised, though, and there's quite a deep cut that will need a good clean, a stitch or two and a dressing. He'll need some anti-inflammatory tablets, too." He glanced up and fixed Amy then Leah with a serious look. "When you factor in the shock, cold and dehydration, you two probably saved his life."

The girls looked at each other. "Really?" gasped Amy. "You are one lucky dog, Scamp!"

"Thank goodness we went up on top of the cliffs," added Leah, "or we'd never have spotted him in the first place."

"On top of the cliffs in a storm?" Mr Ellis cried, looking horrified. "I'll pretend I didn't hear that!"

While Scamp had his paw treated, Amy held him gently but firmly, and Leah stroked him to keep him calm. Then Mr Ellis put a special shoe on his paw that looked like a baseball boot.

"What's that for?" Amy asked.

"It allows him to walk and stops him nibbling at the stitches," the vet explained.

Then it was just a shot of painkiller and antibiotic and they were done.

"What a brave boy!" Amy cooed.

Mr Ellis also scanned for a microchip, but Scamp didn't have one. "I wish I could offer to keep him in our kennels for a few days," he said. "But we're full up at the moment."

"That's OK," said Leah. "I'll get Mum to bring me back and collect him when I've taken Nutmeg home. I'm sure we can look after him until we find his owners." She ruffled Scamp's fur. "You'll like my place, boy. My little brother Adam's a bit annoying, but George is OK, and there are plenty of doggie treats!"

"You girls should be really proud of yourselves, you know," Mr Ellis said.

Amy and Leah thanked him for all his help, and took Scamp back out into reception. Kate insisted that Leah give Rosie a quick ring to check it was fine, and Amy handed Leah her mobile. But as Leah started to speak, Amy saw her face fall.

"But Mum…" Leah was saying. "But that's…" She frowned. "You can't just…"

Amy started to feel worried. Was Rosie saying no? What would happen to Scamp then?

71

"Well, thanks *very* much!" Leah snapped, then stared angrily at the phone. "I can't believe it! She said no!"

"But why?" Amy asked.

"She's got the farrier coming this evening, and it's really busy on the yard tomorrow with a big holiday group arriving for lessons. She says we just can't take on anything else. I told her that I'd look after Scamp myself, but she wouldn't listen." She frowned and pressed redial. "I'm not giving up that easily!"

Kate took the phone gently out of her hand and gave it back to Amy. "Leah, you know your mum would usually say yes," she reasoned. "She really has got a lot on at the moment. Anyway, you must admit that Scamp needs lots of peace and quiet to rest – he's hardly going to get it at your place, is he? Not with Rufus bouncing around, wanting to play."

Leah sighed. "I suppose not."

"I think I'd better call the rescue centre in Castlereach," said Kate.

"Please don't!" Leah begged. "I know they're lovely there. I got Rufus from them, after all. But Scamp's been through a terrible ordeal. Sending him to a new place where he'll be stuck in kennels on his own – I can't bear the thought of it."

"Well, *I* can't take him," said Kate. "You know Smoky's a nightmare with dogs. It looks like the centre's the only option. Unless..."

She and Leah both turned to Amy, who'd
been very quiet since Rosie had said no to
Scamp staying over. Her mind was racing –
like Leah, she hated the thought of Scamp
going to the rescue centre, until he was a
bit better at least. "I'll ask Mum if he can
stay with us," she found herself saying.
"I don't think she'll agree, though."

Nervously, Amy rang Mum and
explained about Scamp and why Leah
couldn't look after him. She couldn't
believe it when Mum agreed that he
could stay, although she did insist that it
was only for one night. When Amy
explained, Leah didn't seem to think that
was a problem. "When she sees how cute
he is, she'll let him stay as long as he
needs to," she said, ruffling Scamp's coat.

"Hmm, I wouldn't be so sure about that,"
Amy muttered.

Kate vanished into a storeroom for a

moment, and came back with Scamp's tablets and clean dressings for his paw. Then she started giving Amy instructions about when to replace the dressing, and how to get the special boot on and off.

As Kate spoke, Amy felt panic rising in her chest. "Erm, I've never looked after a dog before," she gabbled. "I'm not sure I could get his tablets down him, and you said to stop him pulling the shoe thing off, but how do you do that?" She sighed. Maybe Scamp would be better off at the rescue centre after all…

"I could come and sleep over," Leah offered. "I'm used to this kind of stuff."

"Thanks, Leah," cried Amy. "That would be great! I'll just give Mum another call." She stroked Scamp's ears and he nuzzled into her neck. "Us three will have so much fun, won't we, boy?" She couldn't wait to feed him and cuddle him till he fell asleep. Looking after Scamp would be almost like having a dog of her own!

CHAPTER FIVE

"I am serious about this being just for one night, you know," Mum said firmly, as she drove Amy back to the B&B, with Scamp on her lap. "If you and Leah haven't found the owner by teatime tomorrow, I'll be taking you to Castlereach to drop him off at the rescue place."

"I know, I know." Amy realized there was no point in arguing. Mum had even asked Kate for directions to the rescue centre when she'd picked her up, so Amy knew she was serious.

As soon as they got home, she washed
and changed, then curled up in front of the
TV with Scamp. Luckily, the sofa was still
covered in dust sheets, or Mum would
never have allowed a dog on it.

About an hour later, Rosie dropped Leah
off in their battered Land Rover. She
staggered into the half-decorated hallway
with a dog bed and blankets, food and
bowls, her sleeping bag and a backpack full
of overnight gear. "Hello!" she cried,
dumping the pile of stuff on the floor
beside a stack of paint tins.

"Hello!" said Mum. "Amy, Leah's here!"

"Coming!" Amy hurried into the hallway,
followed by Scamp.

"Mum says she's sorry she had to rush
off," said Leah, as Scamp went limping up
to her. She bent down to give him a big
stroke. "Hello, boy! You've landed on your
feet here, haven't you?"

Mum wrinkled up her nose – Amy could see she wasn't keen on the dog bed and blankets. Even she had to admit they were a bit whiffy – Leah must have taken them directly out from under Rufus! "Welcome to East Reach House," Mum said to Leah. "Luxury ensuite B&B accommodation. Well it will be once the builders finally finish!"

"This place is amazing!" Leah enthused. "I like those big pot things over there."

Mum smiled. "Thank you," she said. "They're urns. I'm going to put them either side of the front door, with miniature orange trees in. The people I bought this place from left them here. It must have been very grand as a family house – goodness knows what they did with eight bedrooms! Now, Amy, why don't you show Leah up to your room and help her sort her things out. Off you go, I'll get supper on."

They turned back to Leah's pile of stuff and couldn't help laughing when they saw that Scamp had curled up in the dog bed! "Well, he looks very at home here already!" Leah declared.

Amy lifted Scamp back out of the bed, and picked it up whilst Leah gathered all her stuff. Together they headed up the stairs to Amy's attic bedroom.

When Mum called them for tea she looked a bit dismayed that the smelly dog bed came back down with them, too. Leah put it under the table for Scamp to lie in while they ate their ham and cheese omelettes, but he had other ideas. He jumped on to Amy's lap and refused to move.

Mum rolled her eyes, but she let him stay there, and Amy and Leah fed him scraps of ham when she wasn't looking. Then, while they were helping to wash up, Scamp wolfed down the dinner Leah had brought for him, too. "It's as if he hasn't been fed for a week!" Amy exclaimed.

He didn't need any tablets until the morning, but Leah promised to show Amy how to crush them up into his food at breakfast time.

The girls took Scamp back upstairs with them, and his smelly bed, too – much to

Mum's relief. Even though it was still early, they got changed straight into their pyjamas, so it would feel like the start of the sleepover.

Leah had brought a dog brush with her and, while they were chatting, Amy brushed Scamp until all the mud was out of his fur.

"He already seems like such a different dog to the soggy, trembling little thing we rescued from the cliff top," Leah said.

"There, you're done," Amy told Scamp, once he was all nice and shiny. "Who's a handsome boy, then?"

Scamp gave a bark and the girls giggled. "Oh, you know you are, do you?" Leah teased.

Amy leaned down to give Scamp a stroke. "Here, you can have Harry," she said, tucking her favourite little teddy in beside him. But Scamp took one look at the teddy and started chewing its ear. "Maybe not!" she squealed, snatching Harry back. She rummaged in the bottom of her wardrobe and found an old trainer. "You can have this instead."

"Hang on a minute," said Leah. "Let's see if he knows any commands. Try telling him to sit first."

Amy held the trainer out in front of her. "Sit," she said softly.

Scamp just put his head on one side and gave her a puzzled look.

Leah giggled. "You've got to mean it!" she told her. "Try again."

Amy tried to look stern. "Sit," she commanded. And Scamp did! Amy made a big fuss of him and gave him the trainer.

"Well done," said Leah. "See, you've got to be firm with dogs."

Amy couldn't help giggling. "What, like you are with Rufus?" she teased. "Because he's so obedient – NOT!"

Leah grinned. "Rufus is a special case," she said proudly. "He's practically unteachable. That's what the lady who took his training classes said, anyway!"

"He's so friendly, though," said Amy. "That's what really matters." She sighed. "Oh, I wish I had my own dog! But Mum will never agree to it."

"You were sure she wouldn't agree to Scamp staying over," Leah pointed out, "but here he is. If you just keep showing her how much you love dogs, and take every chance to prove that you can care for one, like you are tonight, then maybe…"

"Maybe," Amy echoed. Scamp dropped the trainer and leaped up on to the bed. He snuggled up next to her and sighed happily. Unfortunately, just at that moment, Mum walked in.

"I've made you some popcorn—" she began, and then she saw Scamp. "Amy, get that dog off the bed!" she shrieked. Scamp sat up, his wagging tail beating up and down on the duvet. He gave her his cutest look, wide-eyed, with his head to one side.

"Please, Mum!" said Amy.

"No!" she cried, shielding her eyes.
"I'm not even looking at that sweet little
face! Get him off there now!"

She put down the bowl of popcorn,
closed her eyes and pretended to stagger
out of the room without looking at Scamp.

Reluctantly, Amy put him back in his
own bed and he got on with chewing the
old trainer.

"And by the way, when you take him out
to do his business, don't think he's doing it
on my new lawn," Mum called from the
hallway. "You'll have to go down to the grass
verge at the end of the road."

"But, Mum, we're in our PJs!" Amy
protested.

Leah laughed. "Shall we go now?" she
asked. "Get it over with?"

Amy and Leah were in fits of giggles, standing on the corner in their pyjamas and slippers, with coats over the top. It was even worse when Amy had to pick up Scamp's poo. She could barely stand up she was laughing so much. "Urgh! The smell!" she gasped, tying up the bag.

"It's all part of having a dog, you know," said Leah. "Anyway, it's not as bad as Rufus's ones. They're huge!"

When Amy and Leah got back, they settled Scamp in his bed. Then Leah got into her sleeping bag and Amy snuggled up under her duvet. Soon they were whispering stories to each other by the light of Leah's torch. Amy wasn't sure if she quite believed Leah's tales about the adventures she and Rufus had had around White Horse Bay, but they were exciting to listen to all the same.

"We've already got our own mystery," Amy said, when Leah's tale of finding a smugglers' map had come to an end. "The mystery of the cliff-top dog. How are we going to find Scamp's owners if they don't want to be found?"

"We'll have to make some posters," Leah said. "And we can ask all over the village tomorrow while we're putting them up."

"Yeah," said Amy. "And you never know, we might even spot the owners ourselves, if they're still looking for Scamp."

"We'll find them, I'm sure of it," said Leah.

"I hope so," said Amy.

Eventually Leah fell asleep, but Amy was far too excited to drift off. Sure that Mum was tucked up in bed by now, she lifted Scamp up on to her pillow. He snuggled into her, and she gave him a big cuddle and told him how gorgeous and special and brave he was.

"I wish I could keep you," she whispered, "but there's no way Mum will let me. If she even finds out you're back on my bed there'll be trouble! And, anyway, I'm sure your owners are missing you like mad. There must be a good reason why they didn't leave their details anywhere. Don't worry, though, Leah and I will track them down for you, whatever it takes."

Scamp licked her face, as if to say thank you. Then he flopped his head on to her arm. And a little while after that, they both fell asleep.

CHAPTER SIX

First thing in the morning, Leah and a
yawning Amy sat down to make some
"Found Dog" posters. Mum was giving
them until five o'clock sharp to find
Scamp's owners, or they were off to
the rescue centre.

"Smile, Scamp!" Amy instructed,
snapping a photo with the camera on her
phone. Dad had made her promise to take
pictures of everything, so he could see what
her new life in White Horse Bay was like.
She was planning to email some to Lucy

and Aisha, too, when she got a chance.

Amy began to upload the picture on to Mum's laptop to create a poster. "I'll just draw it out first, though," she decided, "so we can work out exactly what we want to say."

"Good idea," said Leah, helping herself to another bacon roll from the plate on the kitchen table and sharing it with Scamp.

Amy grabbed her sketchbook from the dresser and riffled through to find a clean page. But then one of the pictures made her pause. The sketch was of a St Bernard, loping along next to its owner. But that wasn't what had caught her eye. "Oh my gosh, Leah, look!" she gasped. "It's Scamp! I'm sure it is! I must have sketched him when I was on the beach one day, and I didn't realize I'd done it. He's only in the background, but…"

Leah looked at the drawing. "Well, it's a young cocker spaniel," she said. She peered

more closely at the page. "Hang on, this
doesn't make sense. You've drawn him with
a little boy, and his mum
and dad. If they're
Scamp's owners,
then who are those
teenagers
searching for him?"
Amy frowned.
"Maybe they're
looking for a
completely different dog,"

she suggested. But she wasn't convinced,
and she guessed Leah wasn't, either.

Amy knew what Leah was thinking, even
before she said it. "The teenagers must
have stolen Scamp! Then maybe he got lost
trying to run away from them, back to his
real owners."

"Well, hang on, we don't know that,"
Amy cautioned.

"Amy! It's the only thing that makes any sense!" Leah insisted. "It explains why the teenagers are looking for him, but not giving their details."

"But it doesn't explain why Scamp's real owners *aren't* looking for him," Amy reasoned.

Leah sighed impatiently. "Maybe they *are*!" she cried. "He could have been stolen somewhere else and then brought here. Say in Castlereach or one of the other villages. They might just be looking in the wrong place. I'll ring the rescue centre and let them know we've got him, and ask Kate to alert the other vets in the area. They're the first places you'd try if you'd lost a dog, aren't they?"

"And we can give them all my mobile number, so we'll know straight away if anyone comes forward," said Amy. "Meanwhile, let's still ask around the shops in the village. This family has been in White Horse Bay at least once over the last few days, if I sketched them on the beach."

"Yes," said Leah. "Someone might have seen them, or know where they're staying."

"Oh, if only I'd had the family in the foreground instead of that St Bernard!" Amy cried. "They're tiny – no one's going to recognize them by looking at this!"

"Maybe not," Leah admitted, "but thanks to your sketch we know we're asking about a mum, dad and little boy, and they'll have been with Scamp, of course. That's quite a lot to go on."

"True," said Amy. "And we should still make some 'Found Dog' posters to put up around the village. If our theory's right, the real owners might see one and contact us."

Leah's eyes gleamed. "Or the thieves might see one and ring the number. They don't know that *we* know Scamp was stolen.

94

We could set a trap and let them walk right into it. Then we can turn them in for dognapping!"

Amy wasn't sure about that. She didn't fancy a run-in with a group of teenagers. Anyone who could steal a dog had to be pretty nasty. Who knew what else they might be capable of. But Leah, being Leah, didn't see the danger – only the excitement. Amy decided to go along with her friend's plan for now, but she knew she'd have to keep an eye out for any trouble. "OK, let's go for it," she said.

First Leah called the rescue centre and explained about Scamp. Then she rang Kate, who said she'd contact the rest of the vets in the area for them. After that, the girls clipped Rufus's spare lead on to Scamp's collar and headed into the village. He was OK walking, so long as he took it slowly. In fact, Kate had told them that some light exercise would actually help the swelling in his paw to go down.

The girls walked from one end of the village to the other, up and down every steep hill. Soon Scamp was puffed out and they had to take turns to carry him. They'd been into every shop and café, and all the guesthouses, to ask if they could put up their posters and to find out whether anyone had seen the group of teenagers, or the family in Amy's sketch.

Some of the people they talked to did say
that either a girl, a boy in a red jacket, or
another boy with glasses had been in to ask
about a dog. And they all said that
whenever they'd tried to take their details
or ask more about it, the teenagers had
hurried away. But that just confirmed what
the girls already knew, and no one seemed
to know anything about Scamp's real family.
Amy kept checking her phone, but no one
had called them, either.

Amy and Leah hadn't had any lunch, and
by four o'clock they couldn't ignore their
rumbling tummies any longer, so they
stopped at the Beach Café.

"Any news on Scamp?" asked Mr
Penhale, setting their smoothies and
sandwiches down on the table and stopping
to stroke the dog's ears.

"Not yet, but we've put posters up all
over the village," said Amy.

"And asked everyone we can," added Leah. "You haven't seen those teenagers again today, have you?"

"Sorry, we haven't," he said. He looked at  the poster Leah had pinned on to the noticeboard. "We'll be sure to call you if we do, though," he promised.

Leah took a big slurp of her drink. "We're no closer to solving the mystery than we were yesterday," she said glumly. "And time's running out."

"Let's not give up just yet," Amy urged her. "We've got until five."

"Maybe those teenagers have moved on, without Scamp," Leah said. "What a shame. I wanted to catch them!"

Amy shrugged and shared the last of her prawn mayo sandwich with Scamp. "Maybe it's for the best. Who knows how they might have reacted if they'd seen us with this little one. They could have been dangerous."

"Well, they wouldn't have scared me!" Leah insisted.

Amy sighed. "I don't know where else we can try," she said.

Leah was silent for a moment. "Oh, I've just had a thought," she said. "If Scamp's real owners are staying round here, they might be up at the campsite right on the edge of the village. It's quite a walk, but if we go now…"

"It's worth a try, I suppose." Amy felt as exhausted as Leah did, and she didn't fancy another long trek up a steep hill. But when she looked into Scamp's hopeful face, she was determined to spend every single second they had left trying to find his family.

CHAPTER SEVEN

The campsite was set quite a way back
from the main village, up a narrow lane.
It was at least a twenty-minute walk, and
Amy and Leah hurried along, with Scamp
pattering next to them on his lead.

"Let's take the short cut through the
fields," said Leah, gesturing to a stile on
their left. "That's the way everyone walks
from the site to get to the beach and
village. It's safer than staying on this lane
with the traffic." Sure enough, the couple
who'd been just ahead of them were now

climbing the stile, bags from the village shop in hand.

The girls headed across the field, and then followed the path over another stile into the next one.

"I'm sure we'll find Scamp's owners up here, if they're staying in White Horse Bay," said Leah, as they made their way up to the campsite. "We've tried everywhere else."

Amy nodded. "Or someone might know something about them, at least."

But when they got to the campsite, they found the place almost deserted. Everyone seemed to have gone out for the day, to make the most of the sunshine. The couple they'd followed knew nothing, and the only other people around had just arrived and were still pitching their tent. Leah asked, anyway, but they hadn't seen the teenagers, or the family in the sketch.

Amy glanced at her watch. "It's a quarter

to five," she said. "There's no time to try anywhere else now." She sat down in the grass, pulled Scamp on to her lap and made a big fuss of him. "I'm so sorry but we'll have to take you to the rescue centre after all," she told him sadly. "I'm sure the people there are lovely, but I hate the thought of you having to go somewhere new, without us to look after you." She sighed heavily.

Leah sat down, too, and put her arm round Amy's shoulders. "We've tried our best," she insisted, "and without us, Scamp might not even be here. His owners might still come forward, and even if they don't, well, he's such a gorgeous boy he'll be snapped up by someone new in no time."

Amy smiled. "Thanks for trying to make me feel better," she said. "I suppose we should head back." She put Scamp down and got to her feet.

They were on their way back through the

field closest to the lane when suddenly, Scamp stopped still. "Hey, what's up, boy?" asked Amy. She pulled gently at the lead, but he wouldn't move. She leaned down to have a look. "He's smelling something. No, hang on, he's eating something."

Leah quickly shooed Scamp away. "Leave it!" she cried, then peered down at the patch of grass. "Oh, it's OK. It's only dog treats."

"Look, there's another pile," said Amy, gesturing across the grass. "And another."

"Why would someone leave dog treats here?" Leah wondered aloud.

"Maybe they bought them from the shop and the bag had a hole in," Amy suggested.

Leah frowned. "I don't think so, not unless they were walking all over the field in a big zigzag." Suddenly, her face lit up. "What if they were trying to entice a dog back – one that they'd lost?"

"Leah…" Amy began.

"Maybe we're close to where Scamp ran off in the first place," Leah continued, breathless with excitement. "Because you'd keep looking close by, wouldn't you, in case the dog came back? And the treats must only just have been left here, or another dog would have scoffed them, so Scamp's family are probably still around."

"Or the teenagers," Amy warned.

"Oh, I'm sure they've moved on," Leah said. "No one's seen them today, remember?"

"I hope you're right," said Amy. "I don't fancy running into them out here, when we're all on our own."

"Amy, don't worry, they've gone," Leah insisted. "Anyway, I reckon if we hang on for a while, Scamp's family will come back and check whether he's turned up."

"It's worth a try," Amy agreed. She glanced at her watch. "Let's wait here till five. It's ten to now. Then I really will have to ring Mum."

They waited around for another few minutes, and when no one came by, they began to make their way across the field to the stile. Amy sighed. "Well, I guess it was a long shot," she said. She pulled out her phone from her back pocket.

But then she and Leah both froze as someone came vaulting over the stile. It was a teenage boy in a red jacket, closely followed by a skinny blonde girl and another boy with glasses.

Amy clutched Leah's arm. "It's them –
the dog thieves!" she whispered. "What are
we going to do?"

But Leah didn't reply. Instead she just
glared at them.

The group were staring back at the girls,
pointing at Scamp and muttering to each
other. Her heart pounding, Amy snatched
him up from the ground and hugged him
to her chest.

The three teenagers were coming towards them now. Amy glanced around. High hedges enclosed the field, and the gate that led to the campsite was a long way back. They could make a run for it, but the teenagers would catch them up long before they reached it. Amy looked over at the stile, willing someone else to come over it, so they could ask for help. But no one did.

Leah stared at the teenagers defiantly. "They are NOT taking Scamp," she hissed, as they closed in.

Amy felt sick. "I agree," she whispered. "We can't give him up. But it's just us against three dog thieves. Will we have any choice?"

CHAPTER EIGHT

"Hey, where did you get that dog?" shouted the boy in the red jacket.

Amy held Scamp tight in her trembling arms, while Leah geared up for a row. "We know you stole him from his real owners," she snapped. "And don't even think about trying to take him again, because we'll go straight to the police and we can easily identify you!"

The teenagers were coming closer, hurrying now.

"Amy, call the police!" Leah said. She was

trying to act tough, but her voice was wavering, and Amy knew she was scared, too.

"It *is* Jester!" cried the girl, as she reached Amy. "Oh, thank goodness! Look at your paw, oh, you poor little babe!"

Scamp leaned out of Amy's arms. He planted his paws on the girl's shoulders and started licking her face, his tail wagging frantically. The two boys came over and began to make a fuss of him, too.

"Hey, Jester, where have you been?" asked the boy in the red jacket.

"Yeah, we've been so worried about you!" cried the other boy.

Amy and Leah exchanged puzzled glances, and Amy cuddled Scamp close. "So, you're saying he's *your* dog, then?" asked Leah.

"Of course he is," said the girl. "I don't know what you were on about, saying we'd stolen him." She reached out her arms to take him, but Amy found herself holding on, refusing to hand him over. There were still things that didn't make sense. She had to be sure they really were the owners first... As she coiled the lead round her wrist, the girl frowned. "Hey, what's wrong with you? Give me my dog!"

Amy just stared at her, but Leah stepped in. "No," she said firmly. "Not until we know you're his real owners."

All three of them looked annoyed about that. "This is stupid. Of course he's ours. Now, hand him over," the boy in the red jacket said gruffly.

Amy's heart was banging hard. "No," she said, her voice shaking.

"If he's really yours and you've got nothing to hide, then why didn't you leave contact details at any of the shops and cafés, or at the vet's?" Leah demanded.

The teenagers glanced at each other. Both Amy and Leah instantly saw it on their faces – they looked guilty.

"We don't have to answer to you, you're only a couple of little kids," sneered the boy in the red jacket. "Just give us our dog and there won't be any trouble."

Amy was really scared then. Would they actually have to fight for Scamp?

But Leah was furious. "This isn't a game, you know!" she snapped. "Do you realize what happened to this poor little dog? He fell down the cliffs and got stuck on a ledge. He was there for hours, with an injured paw, no food or water, shocked and freezing cold in a storm! The vet said that if we hadn't got him down when we did, he might have *died*."

The word hung in the air. The three teenagers looked horrified. Then the girl burst into tears. "The cliffs?" she gasped. "What on earth was he doing all the way over there?"

"We're staying at the campsite and we were here in the field, playing with him, when he ran off," said the boy in the red jacket. He didn't seem at all menacing now, just worried. "He *is* Rachel's dog, honestly. Me and Daz, we're her cousins. We've come on holiday with Uncle Bill and Aunt Molly, and Rachel and her little brother Leo."

"We'd taken Jester out while Uncle Bill and Aunt Molly took Leo to the aquarium in Castlereach," said Daz. "He must have got a scent and he ran off and went through a gap in the hedge. We chased after him, of course, but the hedge was so thick, we had to go round by the stile—"

"And by the time we got into the next field, we couldn't see him," Rachel put in, her voice choked with tears.

"We searched and searched, but we couldn't find him anywhere. After a couple of hours looking round here, we had the idea of asking down in the village," Daz added.

Leah and Amy exchanged a glance. They still didn't know whether to believe them.

"So, why all the secrecy?" asked Leah. "Why didn't you leave your details anywhere? If you had, we could have called you and you'd have known he was safe."

Rachel burst into fresh sobs. "It was my fault he got lost," she stuttered. "Dad said not to take him off the lead when we were by ourselves. He's not exactly great about coming back when you call him, and he'd lost his collar tag. That's part of the reason why they went into Castlereach yesterday — to get him a new one."

"No, it's my fault," Daz insisted. "I'm the one who said we should let him have a little run around. Mark wasn't sure, but—"

"I didn't stop you, though," said the other boy. "We just let him off for a few minutes, but then he went haring away."

"Dad's phone is the only one that gets

any reception round here," Rachel explained. "We knew that if we left his number with people and he found out what we'd done, we'd be in so much trouble…"

"Oh, so you were just covering your backs!" Leah accused.

Rachel shook her head. "OK, I admit we were scared of what he'd say. But the main reason was Leo, my little brother. He's crazy about Jester – they're best friends. He'd have been so upset if he knew he was missing."

"We decided the only thing to do was find him ourselves, so Leo didn't have to be told about it," said Daz.

"We looked until dark," Rachel continued. "When we got back, Leo was already asleep – he's only five. I told Mum and Dad that Jester was asleep, too, in Mark and Daz's tent, to explain why I hadn't brought him back in with me. This morning we set out early to start searching again. We left them a note saying we'd gone exploring, and taken Jester with us."

"We walked round the lanes leading out of White Horse Bay, and searched all over the fields," Mark explained.

"So that's why no one in the village has seen you today, and why you haven't seen our posters," Amy said. "Because you went looking in the other direction."

Daz nodded. "We thought, for no one at all to have seen him yesterday... Well, it's only a small village. We convinced ourselves we were looking in the wrong place. None of us ever imagined he could have got up on the cliffs!"

"But we had no luck this morning, either," Mark continued, "and when we stopped in the garage by the main road, I had the idea of buying the dog treats and scattering them where we lost him."

"We were going to have one more look

round these fields and hedges," Daz told them. "And then go back to the campsite and come clean."

"Oh, it's been awful!" Rachel said, with a shudder. "But he's here now. That's what matters. Thank you so much…" She paused and looked questioningly at the girls.

"Amy," said Amy, "and this is Leah."

"Well, thanks, Amy and Leah," said Mark.

"We're really grateful," Daz added. "Without you, well, like you said…" he grimaced and shook his head.

Amy glanced at Leah. She wanted to hand Jester back, but only if her friend agreed. They were in this together, after all. Luckily, Leah nodded.

Amy gave the dog a big cuddle. "Bye, little scamp," she whispered. "Thanks for being my very own dog for a night!"

The dog scrambled up her jacket and gave her face a big lick. Then, feeling a mixture of happiness and sadness, Amy placed him on the ground.

Rachel held on to his collar while Leah unclipped Rufus's lead. Then Rachel brought out Jester's lead and clipped it on.

Leah rummaged in her pocket and handed over the rest of his tablets. "Just one crushed up in his dinner tonight and one tomorrow morning, that's all, and you'll need to take him back to a vet in a week's time for a check-up," she said.

"Thanks so much," said Rachel, grinning. "We'll never do anything so stupid again, I promise. When I think what could have happened... Oh!" she gasped. "Look."

The boys turned round. "Uh-oh," said Daz.

Three people were walking across the field towards them, from the direction of the campsite. It was a man and woman, swinging their little boy between them as they walked along.

"It's Uncle Bill, Aunt Molly and Leo," cried Mark. "How on earth are we going to explain what happened to Jester's paw?"

"I don't know," said Rachel anxiously. She turned to Amy and Leah. "You aren't going to tell them about us losing him, are you?"

CHAPTER NINE

Molly waved as they drew near. "Hi, guys!"
she called. "We had a great time at the
steam railway. I'm glad we've found you!
We're heading into Castlereach tonight for
pizza, if you fancy it?"

"I know it's not cool to hang out with the
olds, but it'll be nice to do *something* all
together!" Bill added.

"Jester!" cried Leo, dashing over.

"Don't worry, we won't tell, will we,
Amy?" said Leah hurriedly.

"No, we won't," Amy promised. There'd

been a moment when she'd felt like it, but with the shock they'd had, she knew they'd got the point.

Jester pulled Rachel over to Leo, and the little boy dropped to the ground to make a big fuss of him.

Amy and Leah grinned at each other. Even if Jester's family would never find out what they'd done for him, the girls knew they'd saved his life, and that was enough.

"This is Amy and Leah," said Rachel, and they all said hello.

"Actually, we're just heading off…" Amy said.

"Hey, what happened to Jester's paw?" asked Molly suddenly.

Rachel, Mark and Daz were all silent for a moment, looking panicked. Then Rachel took a deep breath. "I'm afraid we made a silly mistake…" she began, much to Amy and Leah's surprise. As the group wandered away, with Leo and Jester running ahead, they heard her say, "I don't think you'll want to take us for pizza after you hear this…"

"Wow, she's going to tell them everything after all," said Leah. "She's brave! *My* dad would go mad if it was Rufus!"

"I suppose she knew deep down it was the right thing to do," said Amy. "We really got it wrong about them, didn't we?" she added, with a smile. "Thinking they were dog thieves!"

"A little bit," Leah admitted. "Still, we found Scamp's … I mean, *Jester's* owners in the end, so it all worked out OK."

"Yeah, and just in time, too!" Amy added. She glanced at her watch. "Oh no! It's ten past five!" She pulled out her mobile and called Mum. After explaining about finding Jester's owners, she said yes and no a lot, then hung up. "Mum says well done us!" she told Leah. "And she also said that, as we don't have to go into Castlereach now, she'll treat us to fish and chips on the beach!"

"Your mum's great," Leah exclaimed. "Even if she's not into animals," she added, laughing. "I saw the way she looked at the dog bed last night!"

Amy giggled. "Oh dear, you weren't offended, were you?"

Leah shook her head. "Course not!"

Amy smiled wickedly. "Good. In that case I admit I found it a bit whiffy, too!"

"Oy! Are you saying my dog smells?" Leah teased, as they made their way back over the stile and headed down the lane.

Half an hour later, Leah, Amy and Mum were sitting on the sand eating their fish and chips out of the white paper wrapping. Leah told Amy's mum the whole story of the teenagers, the family in the sketch and the not-stolen-after-all dog, with Amy chipping in now and then. Leah hadn't mentioned that they'd been on the cliff top in the storm, and Amy decided that it was best left for another day, when she and Mum were on their own.

"Well done," Mum said. She held up her can of lemonade. "To Amy and Leah, the brave mystery solvers!"

They clinked their cans with hers. "To us!"

"Now, how am I supposed to eat with this thing?" asked Mum, as another chip fell off the tiny wooden fork she'd been given and rolled down her shirt. "I'm getting in an awful mess!"

"Just pick them up with your fingers," said Leah.

Mum shrugged and tried it. "Oh yes, much easier!"

"Look, it's your brother and Rufus," cried Amy, as Leah's dog came bounding towards them. Mum leaped to her feet as he approached, obviously not keen on a wet-nosed greeting from a shaggy dog!

"Hi," said George.

"Hi," they all chorused.

"Yum, fish and chips, good idea. Leah, you watch Rufus, and I'll go and get some, too."

Leah gave her dog a big fuss and cuddle as her brother strode off. "Hey!" she cried, as Rufus shoved his nose into her chips.

"Oh, I wish I had a dog," Amy sighed.

Mum laughed. "Really! I had no idea. You've never mentioned it before!"

"Ha ha!" cried Amy, nudging her arm. Mum nudged her back and then pulled her into a hug.

"Come on," said Leah to Amy, picking up a piece of driftwood. "Let's throw this in the water for Rufus."

The girls wandered down to the shoreline and took turns to hurl the driftwood into the waves. Rufus gave an excited bark every time and bounded in after it.

"Mum's right, you were really brave. I still can't believe you climbed up that cliff to reach Jester," Amy said.

Leah shuddered. "It was terrifying. I can't believe I did it now, looking back. But at the time all I could think about was rescuing him. And anyway, if it hadn't been for your quick thinking about the bridle and the warm jacket, he might not have survived."

"Maybe," Amy said. She had to admit to feeling just a little bit proud of herself.

"We're a great team," said Leah. "Whenever animals need help, we'll be there!"

"Yes! We're…" Amy thought for a moment. "Animal S.O.S!"

"I like it!" Leah exclaimed. "I wonder what our next adventure will be? Hey, George is back. Let's go and pinch some of his chips. I've finished all mine."

The two friends grinned at each other and, with Rufus bouncing along beside them, they linked arms and headed back up the beach.

Take a peek at the first chapter
of Amy and Leah's next adventure:

THE HAUNTED HOUSE
KITTENS

CHAPTER ONE

Amy staggered into her friend Leah's front
hall, loaded up with all her sleepover stuff.

"Wow, are you staying for a week?" joked
Rosie, Leah's mum, as Amy put it all down.

"Hi, Amy!" cried Leah, rushing in from
the stable yard and pulling off her boots.
"Gosh, what a lot of jumpers!"

Amy grinned at the pile on the floor.
"Mum insisted. She says it'll be chilly in
the barn overnight."

"She's right," said Rosie. "Are you sure you
girls wouldn't rather sleep in the house?"

"No way!" cried Leah. "Sleeping out is much more fun. Oooh, what's in there?"

Amy took the lid off the big round tin she was clutching, to reveal a dozen cupcakes with stars sprinkled on top.

"Wow!" gasped Leah.

"They look delicious," Rosie said.

Just then, Leah's little brother, Adam, came down the stairs. "Hey, are those for me?" he asked cheekily, without even saying hello.

He marched up and tried to reach into the tin, but Leah pushed his hand away. "Get out, pig! These are for our sleepover!"

"I'll put them in the kitchen," Rosie told Amy. "Leah, don't forget you've still got chores to finish on the yard."

"I'll give you a hand," said Amy.

As they made their way across to the stables, Leah's dog, Rufus, bounded over to join them. Amy ruffled his brown shaggy fur as he jumped up at her.

"Down, boy!" said Leah firmly. Of course, Rufus took absolutely no notice. "How is your getting-a-dog campaign going?" she asked Amy.

Amy shrugged. "I've mentioned it a few times, but Mum's so busy with the builders she hardly has time to think about anything else. The B&B opens in six weeks, so she's in a mad rush to get everything finished. And once it's all perfect, she's even less likely to want a dog jumping all over things…"

"Hmm, tricky," said Leah. She grabbed the wheelbarrow that was leaning up against the side of the tack room and loaded two forks on to it. Then she and Amy went over to Nutmeg and Gracie's stables.

Amy gave Gracie a pat and stroke as she led her out and tied her up by the door, and Gracie nudged her affectionately with her muzzle. Amy had ridden the pony in her last lesson and she was already mad about her. As she and Leah mucked out the stables, Amy could almost pretend that the gentle grey mare was actually hers.

"I can't wait till we can go out on hacks together," she told Leah. "I've got the hang of rising trot now, and I hope I'll get a go at canter soon."

"You're doing really well," said Leah. "Mum says you're a natural."

Amy blushed, but couldn't help grinning. "Thanks. I've dreamed of riding all my life – it's amazing that I'm actually getting the chance to learn. Honestly, you don't know how lucky you are living at a stables!"

"Yeah, cos I get to do this all day!" Leah joked, holding up a forkful of pony poo.

Leah's dad, Dan, and her big brother, George, came out to help them finish off the evening chores. When everything was done, the girls headed back in to gather up their things for the sleepover.

"Don't forget those yummy cakes!" said Leah, as they went into the kitchen.

"How about we each have one now? We deserve it after all that mucking out!"

"Definitely," Amy agreed, pulling off the lid of the cake tin. "Hey, there are two missing!"

"Adam! I should have known he'd do something like this!" Leah cried. "Wait till I get my hands on him! No, hang on..." she said, with a cheeky grin. "I've got a better idea."

Amy giggled as Leah reached up to the spice rack on the wall and took down a jar of chilli flakes. "I like your thinking!"

Leah got out a butter knife and carefully lifted the icing on one of the cakes just enough to hide a sprinkling of chilli flakes beneath it. Then she left it temptingly on the counter.

The girls made a flask of hot chocolate and were searching the kitchen cupboards for snacks when Rosie came in and put the kettle on. "Oh, Amy, I forgot to ask," she said, as she took a mug from the drainer, "how was your Easter weekend?"

"Great, thanks," said Amy. "I spent it with Dad in London. It was lovely to have four whole days together. We went to see a new exhibition at the Tate Modern. Dad's really into art, like me."

"Well, you're in good company in White Horse Bay," said Rosie. She gestured to a print on the wall. "Samuel Trevelyan lived in this area. That picture is of White Horse Beach."

Amy had a long look at the painting. "There's my favourite spot on the sand to sit and sketch," she told them, pointing it out. "And look, Leah, isn't that the part of the cliffs where we rescued Jester, the stranded dog?"

Leah peered at the picture, too. "Oh, yeah. I've never really looked at it properly before."

"I've heard of Samuel Trevelyan," Amy said to Rosie. "Dad and I went to an exhibition of sea paintings last year. I think I saw a picture of his there."

Just then, Adam appeared, looking very pleased with himself. Leah and Amy were careful to act as if they didn't know anything about the stolen cakes. Rosie sent him to get ready for bed and they pretended not to notice as he swiped the cupcake off the counter on his way out.

Dan and George came in from the yard then and started raiding the cupboards for snacks, too.

"Hey, we bagsied the Jaffa Cakes!" Leah cried, snatching the box back from George.

"Never mind," said Dan, handing him a packet of chocolate digestives, "we'll have to make do with these."

"You only had tea two hours ago!" Rosie sighed. Then they heard a loud yell from upstairs. Leah and Amy burst into giggles. "What's going on?" asked Rosie suspiciously.

"Ask Adam!" Leah smirked. "Come on, Amy, let's go and set up camp!"

Before long, the girls were snuggled in their sleeping bags (and three jumpers each) on bales of hay in the barn. Tiger, the old farm cat, purred softly beside them. They scoffed all the cakes and biscuits as they chatted, and soon it was pitch-dark apart from the security lights shining in

the yard. Dan came to check on them at
about eleven o'clock, just before he and
Rosie went off to bed.

"I hope you girls are going to get some
sleep…" he began.

"Course we are," said Leah. "Definitely
some. A few minutes' worth at least!"

Dan raised his eyebrows. "Goodnight,
Amy," he said, "and you, Trouble."

The girls grinned and said goodnight.

As he headed back to the house, Leah
whispered, "Do you want to hear a ghost
story? I know one that'll scare your socks off."

"What, all four pairs of them?" Amy joked. Her heart was already racing, though. She wasn't great with ghost stories as it was, and out in the open, in the middle of the night…

But Leah had started, and there was no stopping her. "There's a creepy old manor house set on a hill high above White Horse Bay…" she began. Slowly, the story of the Victorian lady of Greystone Manor, who was terrible to everyone – her servants, children and even her pets – began to unfold.

"She fell down the stairs and died, but with her last breath she vowed never to allow anyone to enjoy the house again. And she's haunted it to this day," Leah breathed. "A family did move in, the Mallorys, and stayed for quite a few years, but bad luck befell them at every turn. The daughter moved to Australia to get as far away as possible from the place and the husband died a mysterious death. The wife was eventually driven out by the ghost, who passed her on the staircase every day and appeared each night by her bed to terrify her out of her wits. Now the manor is a ruin…"

Amy shuddered. "Oh, that's horrible!"

"Yeah, really terrifying!" Leah whispered, her voice full of excitement. "Wouldn't it be amazing if someone could get a photo of the ghost, and actually prove the story was true?"

Amy felt her stomach flip. "Oh no, Leah—" she began.

But Leah was off, chatting away about a ghost hunt. "Another mystery for us to investigate!" she cried. "It'll be a fantastic adventure."

"Hmm," said Amy. To her it sounded exactly the opposite.

"Your phone takes photos, doesn't it?" Leah asked eagerly.

Amy nodded. "But, Leah, I don't—"

"Then we can go straight from here tomorrow morning," Leah went on. "You've already cleared it with your mum to spend the day here, haven't you?"

Amy nodded reluctantly.

"Great. We can tell Mum we're just taking Nutmeg for a hack. I think he's got a lesson first thing, but we can set off straight after that. And you can ride my bike…"

In the end Amy agreed to go up to Greystone Manor the next day, just to get Leah off the subject of ghosts. A little later Leah dropped off to sleep, but poor Amy lay awake for ages, listening to the unfamiliar noises around them and jumping every time a gate rattled in the wind. Eventually, she pulled the sleeping bag right up over her head and finally managed to fall asleep.

To find out more about Kelly McKain,
visit her website:

www.kellymckain.co.uk